About this book

This book is for everyone who is learning their first words in Spanish. By looking at the pictures, it will be easy to read and remember the Spanish words underneath.

When you look at the Spanish words, you will see that in front of most of them, there is **la** or **el**, which means "the". When learning Spanish, it is a good idea to learn the **la** or **el** with each word. This is because all Spanish words, like book and table, as well as boy and girl, are masculine or feminine. **La** means the word is feminine and **el** usually means that it is masculine. If the word is plural, that is, there is more than one such as tables or books, then it has **las** or **los** in front of it. **Las** is the feminine and **los** is the masculine.

Some of the words have an n with a squiggle over it, like this ñ. The squiggle is called a tilde. In Spanish this ñ is a separate letter in the alphabet and is said differently from the ordinary **n**. Some letters have accents on them. This does not change the sound of the letter but changes the way the word is said.

At the back of the book is a guide to help you say the words in the pictures. But there are some sounds in Spanish which are quite different from any sounds in English. To say them correctly, you have to hear someone say them, listen very carefully and try to say them that way yourself. But if you say them as they are written in the guide, a Spanish person will understand you — even if your Spanish accent is not quite perfect.

THE FIRST HUNDRED WORDS IN SPANISH

Heather Amery
Illustrated by Stephen Cartwright

Translation and Pronunciation Guide: Jane Stalker

There is a little yellow duck to find in every picture.

En la sala In the living room

el papá
Daddy

la mamá
Mommy

el niño
boy

la niña
girl

la bebé
baby

el perro
dog

el gato
cat

Vestirse Getting dressed

la camiseta
undershirt

la braguita
underwear

los zapatos
shoes

los calcetines
socks

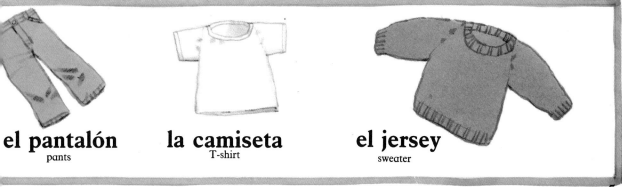

el pantalón
pants

la camiseta
T-shirt

el jersey
sweater

En la cocina In the kitchen

el pan
bread

la leche
milk

los huevos
eggs

la manzana
apple

la naranja
orange

el plátano
banana

Lavar los platos Doing the dishes

la mesa
table

la silla
chair

el plato
plate

cuchillo
knife

el tenedor
fork

la cuchara
spoon

la taza
cup

La hora del juego _{Play time}

el caballo
horse

la oveja
sheep

la vaca
cow

10

la gallina
hen

el cerdo
pig

el tren
train

los ladrillos
blocks

Hacer la visita Going on a visit

la abuela
Grandma

el abuelo
Grandpa

las zapatillas
slippers

el vestido
dress

el abrigo
coat

la gorra
hat

13

En el parque In the park

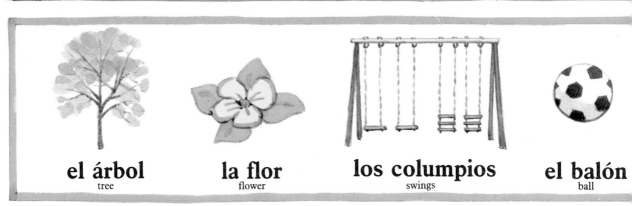

el árbol
tree

la flor
flower

los columpios
swings

el balón
ball

el tobogán
slide

el pájaro
bird

las botas
boots

el barco
boat

Por la calle In the street

el coche
car

la bicicleta
bicycle

la camioneta
truck

el autobús
bus

el avión
airplane

la casa
house

Celebrar una fiesta Having a party

el helado
ice cream

la tarta
cake

el globo
balloon

el reloj
clock

el pez
fish

las galletas
cookies

los caramelos
candy

Nadar Swimming

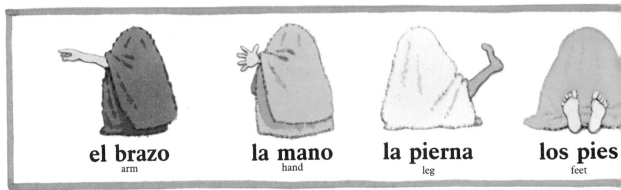

el brazo
arm

la mano
hand

la pierna
leg

los pies
feet

s dedos de los pies
toes

la cabeza
head

el culo
bottom

la boca
mouth

los ojos
eyes

las orejas
ears

22

la nariz
nose

el cabello
hair

el peine
comb

el cepillo
brush

rojo
red

azúl
blue

verde
green

amarillo
yellow

rosado
pink

blanco
white

negro
black

En el cuarto de baño In the bathroom

la bañera
bathtub

la toalla
towel

el wáte
toilet

el jabón
soap

la barriguita
tummy

el pato
duck

En el dormitorio In the bedroom

la cama
bed

la ventana
window

la puerta
door

lamparilla
light

el libro
book

la muñeca
doll

el osito
teddy

Match the words to the pictures

el balón

las botas

los calcetines

la camiseta

el cerdo

el coche

el cuchillo

el gato

la gorra

el helado

el huevo

el jersey

la lamparilla

la leche

el libro

la manzana

la mesa

la muñeca

la naranja

el osito

el pato

el perro

el pez

el plátano

el reloj

la tarta

el tenedor

el tren

la vaca

la ventana

31

Contar Counting

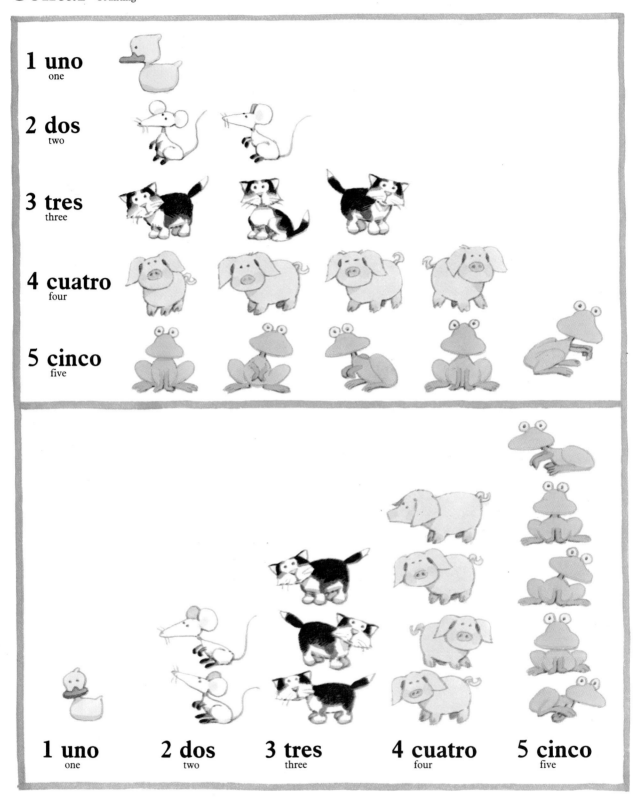

1 **uno** one

2 **dos** two

3 **tres** three

4 **cuatro** four

5 **cinco** five

1 **uno** one 2 **dos** two 3 **tres** three 4 **cuatro** four 5 **cinco** five

First published in 1988. © Usborne Publishing Ltd. Printed in Great Britain. American edition 1988.

Words in the pictures

In this alphabetical list of all the words in the pictures, the Spanish word comes first, next is the guide to saying the word, and then there is the English translation. The guide may look strange, but just try to read it as if it were English words. It will help you to say the words in Spanish correctly if you remember these rules.

Capital, or BIG, letters show which part of the word to stress
a is like *a* in h*a*ppen
e is like *e* in h*e*lp
o is like *o* in h*o*rse
ch is quite different from any sound in English but is like the *ch* in the Scottish word *loch*
rrr is *r* rolled on your tongue, like the *r* in the name of Scottish poet *Burns*
th is like the *th* in mo*th*

abrigo	*aBREEgo*	coat
abuela	*aBWEla*	Grandma
abuelo	*aBWElo*	grandpa
amarillo	*amaREELyo*	yellow
autobús	*aootoBOOSS*	bus
avión	*abeeONN*	airplane
azul	*aTHOOL*	blue
balón	*baLONN*	ball
bañera	*baNYEra*	bathtub
barco	*BARko*	boat
barriguita	*bareeGEEta*	tummy
bebé	*beBE*	baby
bicicleta	*beetheeKLEta*	bicycle
blanco	*BLANko*	white
boca	*BOka*	mouth
botas	*BOtass*	boots
braguita	*braGEEta*	underwear
brazo	*BRAtho*	arm
caballo	*kaBALyo*	horse
cabello	*kaBELyo*	hair
calcetines	*kaltheTEEness*	socks
calle	*KALye*	street
cama	*KAma*	bed
camioneta	*kameeoNEta*	truck
camiseta	*kameeSSEta*	undershirt, T-shirt
caramelos	*karaMEloss*	candy
casa	*KAssa*	house
cepillo	*thePEELyo*	brush
cerdo	*THERdo*	pig
cinco	*THEENko*	five
cocina	*koTHEEna*	kitchen

coche	*KOTshe*	car
columpios	*koLOOMpyoss*	swings
compras	*KOMprass*	shopping
cuarto de baño	*kwartodeBANyo*	bathroom
cuatro	*KWAtro*	four
cuchara	*kootSHAra*	spoon
cuchillo	*kootSHEELyo*	knife
culo	*KOOlo*	bottom
dedos de los pies	*dedoss-delossPYESS*	toes
dormitorio	*dormeeTORyo*	bedroom
dos	*doss*	two
fiesta	*FYESSta*	party
flor	*flor*	flower
galletas	*galYEtass*	cookies
gallina	*galYEEna*	hen
gato	*GAto*	cat
globo	*GLObo*	balloon
gorra	*GOrrra*	hat
helado	*eLAdo*	ice cream
huevos	*WEboss*	eggs
jabón	*chaBONN*	soap
jersey	*cherSSEY*	sweater
juego	*CHWEgo*	game
ladrillos	*laDREELyoss*	blocks
lamparilla	*lampaREELya*	light
leche	*LETshe*	milk
libro	*LEEbro*	book

mamá	*maMA*	Mommy		puerta	*PWERta*	door
mano	*MAno*	hand				
manzana	*manTHAna*	apple		reloj	*rreLOCH*	clock
mesa	*MEssa*	table		rojo	*RRROcho*	red
muñeca	*mooNYEka*	doll		rosado	*roSSAdo*	pink
naranja	*naRANcha*	orange		sala	*SSAla*	living room
nariz	*naREETH*	nose		silla	*SSEELya*	chair
negro	*NEgro*	black		tarta	*TARta*	cake
niña	*NEENya*	girl		taza	*TAtha*	cup
niño	*NEENyo*	boy		tenedor	*teneDOR*	fork
				toalla	*toALya*	towel
ojos	*ochos*	eyes		tobogán	*toboGANN*	slide
orejas	*oREchas*	ears		tren	*trenn*	train
osito	*oSEEto*	teddy		tres	*tress*	three
oveja	*oBEcha*	sheep				
				uno	*OOno*	one
pájaro	*PAcharo*	bird				
pan	*pann*	bread		vaca	*BAka*	cow
pantalón	*pantaLONN*	pants		ventana	*benTAna*	window
papá	*paPA*	Daddy		verde	*BERde*	green
parque	*PARke*	park		vestido	*besTEEdo*	dress
pato	*PAto*	duck		vestidor	*besteeDOR*	changing room
peine	*PEYne*	comb				
perro	*PErro*	dog		visita	*beeSEEta*	visit
pez	*peth*	fish				
pierna	*PYERna*	leg		wáter	*WAter*	toilet
pies	*pyess*	feet				
plátano	*PLAtano*	banana		zapatillas	*thapaTEELyas*	slippers
plato	*PLAto*	plate		zapatos	*thaPAtoss*	shoes

First published in 1988. Usborne Publishing Ltd, 20 Garrick Street, WC2E 9BJ, England. © Usborne Publishing Ltd, 1988.

Printed in Great Britain. American edition 1988